A.P.J. Abdul Kalam
Scientist and Humanist

A.P.J. Abdul Kalam
Scientist and Humanist

Atulindra Nath Chaturvedi

RUPA
PUBLICATIONS INDIA

Copyright © Atulindra Nath Chaturvedi 2002

First Published 2002
First in Rupa Paperback 2012

Published by
Rupa Publications India Pvt. Ltd.
7/16, Ansari Road, Daryaganj,
New Delhi 110 002

Sales Centres:

Allahabad Bengaluru Chennai
Hyderabad Jaipur Kathmandu
Kolkata Mumbai

All rights reserved.
No part of this publication may be reproduced, stored in a
retrieval system, or transmitted, in any form or by any
means, electronic, mechanical, photocopying, recording or
otherwise, without the prior permission of the publishers.

The author asserts the moral right to be identified
as the author of this work.

Printed in India by
Nutech Photolithographers
B-240, Okhla Industrial Area, Phase-I,
New Delhi 110 020, India

Contents

Introduction	vii
Chapter 1: The Making of a Scientist	1
Chapter 2: Rocket Man	11
Chapter 3: The Mission of Self-Reliance	21
Chapter 4: The Unexpected President	30
Chapter 5: The Man And His Vision	38
Envoi	45
The Election Manifesto	46
The Vision of India	60
Chronology	68
A Bibliographic Note	70
Author's Profile	72

Introduction

Science and technology are not something new to India. The list is long, from Aryabhatta and Varahamira to C.V. Raman, J.C. Bose, S. Chandrasekhar, and Vikram Sarabhai. Avul Pakir Jainulabdeen Abdul Kalam can justly lay claim to this great heritage. He is a practical scientist, pushing himself to excellence, and inspiring others to give their best. The result is the great contribution he made to India's defence programme. But he is more than just a scientist. He has allied his knowledge and understanding of the potential of science and technology with an energising vision for the development of India and her people. It is this vision that propelled him into the office of President. It is for this reason we call him Dr Kalam, Scientist and Humanist – truly a Bharat Ratna, the jewel of India.

Kalam's Father Jainulabdeen

Chapter 1
The Making of a Scientist

To live only for some unknown future is superficial
— *A.P.J. Abdul Kalam*

Rameswaram is a small town, an island off the coast of the southern Indian state of Tamil Nadu. The life of the town continues to centre around the temple dedicated to Shiva, as it has for centuries. It is said that the temple stands at the spot where Sri Rama worshipped Shiva – an act of reconciliation between the warring followers of Vishnu and Shiva. If it is a coincidence

Kalam's home on Mosque Street

that Abdul Kalam was born here, on 15 October 1931, in the very place of conciliation, then it is certainly a divine one, given that his appeal transcends all barriers of caste and community.

A short distance away lies Dhanushkodi. It is here that the family of Abdul Kalam lived. His father, Jainulabdeen Marakayar, was born in 1874. His mother was Ashiamma. Jainulabdeen was not an educated man, and his wife came from a family which had a higher social standing. Jainulabdeen earned his living as a boatman, ferrying pilgrims to Rameswaram.

Though the family did not have much money, Kalam, one of three brothers and a sister, never felt that he had been deprived either emotionally or materially.

Jainulabdeen may have been uneducated, but he had learned his lessons in the hard school of life. These he passed on to his young son. According to Kalam, he learned honesty and self-discipline from his father. From his mother, he acquired the need to have faith in others and the importance of kindness in one's life.

Jainulabdeen, a devout Muslim, was a close friend of Pandit Lakshman Sastry, the head priest of the Rameswaram temple. This was quite an extraordinary situation, given the sharp religious and social divisions prevalent then. Among Kalam's earliest memories are those of his father and Sastry discussing religious issues. One of the precepts that Kalam learned early in life was the importance of transcending all issues that divide man from man. Discussing the importance of prayer, Jainulabdeen told his son: 'When you pray, you transcend your body and become a part of the cosmos, which knows no wealth, age, or creed.'

Kalam felt the full force of discrimination when a new teacher, unable to reconcile himself to seeing a Hindu and a Muslim boy sitting together, brusquely told him to go to the backbench. Kalam learned another lesson when Sastry, who was the father of the Hindu boy, summoned the teacher and told him to either mend his ways or leave. Another teacher, Sivasubramanian Iyer, invited Kalam to tea. Iyer's orthodox wife refused to serve Kalam, and Iyer had to do it himself. Iyer invited

The temple of Shiva at Rameswaram

Kalam to dinner the following week, and this time, his wife served dinner.

The two most important formative influences on Kalam were his cousin, Samsuddin, and Ahmed Jallaluddin, who married Kalam's sister, Zohara. Jallaluddin helped Jainulabdeen to repair his boats after a storm, and became closely associated with the family. Jallaluddin was the only person in the area who knew English, and earned a living by writing letters for other people. He took the young boy for long walks, speaking to him of educated people and opening his eyes to the wonders, achievements and importance of modern science.

Samsuddin held the monopoly on the newspaper trade in Rameswaram. Kalam would try to slowly trace in *Dinmani* the news stories that Samsuddin told him. Even today Kalam remembers the first pay that he earned, helping Samsuddin collect the newspaper packets thrown from the train, when it began to bypass the Rameswaram station during the Second World War. He also made money selling tamarind seeds – which, for some reason, were in short supply – at the temple.

Pandit Lakshman Sastry

Kalam's restless young mind was also enchanted by the world of books. He could be found ensconced at all hours of day and night in the library of S.T.R. Manickam, who had once been active in the revolutionary movement against British rule and had retired to Rameswaram.

Sooner or later, the paradise of childhood had to end. With his father's blessings that he become a district

S.T.R. Manickam (inset) at whose house Kalam discovered books

collector, Kalam went to study at Schwartz School in nearby Ramanathapuram, from where, in 1950, he went on to join St Joseph's College at Tiruchirapalli. He graduated with a degree in science from there. At some point, he realised that his interest did not lie in physics and he decided to pursue engineering at the prestigious Madras Institute of Technology (MIT). This, however, was an expensive proposition, even with the scholarship that Kalam had got as he figured on the merit list. His family came to the rescue. Sister Zohara sold her jewellery and gave Kalam the required money.

Kalam spent hours looking at two dismantled planes which were displayed at MIT. They brought back memories of the flying birds he once watched

A view of Schwartz High School

as a child. It was perhaps this childhood memory that influenced his decision to specialise in aeronautical engineering in his second year.

In his third year, Kalam was part of a four-man team given the task of designing a low-level fighter plane. Kalam's job was to design the aerodynamics of the plane. The design was rejected, and Kalam's work was singled out for harsh criticism. He was told by MIT Director, Srinivasan, to give a fresh design within three days; otherwise his scholarship would be stopped. Kalam worked day and night, and on the last day found Srinivasan standing at his shoulder. The new design was accepted and Srinivasan praised him highly. The episode was pivotal for Kalam: he learned

Kalam's inspiring teachers at Schwartz High School, Iyadurai Solomon (standing, Left) and Ramakrishna Iyer (sitting, right)

Kalam's brother with the T-square that Kalam used in his studies

that he should always give his best effort, and never settle for second best.

In 1958, he joined Hindustan Aeronautics Limited (HAL) at Bangalore as a trainee, where he was given a hands-on education in the actual manufacture of an aircraft. He left HAL impressed by the perfectionism of the engineers, the product of years of doing the same task over and over.

A rare moment with the family

He now stood at crossroads. He had two options before him – becoming a pilot in the Indian Air Force, or a scientist in the Directorate of Technical Development and Production (Air) (DTDP), a defence organisation. The Directorate's test was easy, but in the Air Force test at Dehra Dun, Kalam secured the ninth place out of 25 candidates. And only eight were selected.

Dejected, he went to Rishikesh, where he met

Swami Stvananda

Swami Sivananda – a man, in Kalam's words, 'who looked like Buddha'. Unfazed at hearing his Muslim name, the Swami asked him why he was dejected. On being told the reason, he told the young scientist that it was not his destiny to join the Air Force. He told Kalam, 'Forget this failure, it was essential to lead you to your true path.' On reaching Delhi, Kalam found that he had got the DTDP job. It was as if Swami Sivananda's prophecy was coming true.

Chapter 2
Rocket Man

We should not give up, and allow the problem to defeat us
— *A. P. J. Abdul Kalam*

Destiny had played the first of her many games with Kalam. Looking back in later years, he must have thought of his failure to get into the Air Force as providential. For, though he did not get to fly, he was to engage in activity far more interesting, and be a participant in momentous events.

After a short period of training at Kanpur, Kalam was part of a team that developed a DART target. He was soon transferred to Bangalore, where he joined the newly-established Aeronautical Development Establishment (ADE). At first the workload was light, and Kalam had to scrounge around and find something to do on his own. However, after a year, work began to flow in.

M.G.K. Menon

A project team was set up to design and develop the prototype of an indigenous hovercraft, known as a Ground Equipment Machine. The team was given a three-year period to make the model airborne. According to Kalam, the attempt 'opened the windows of my mind' to the possibilities of developing ideas. After a working model was produced, Defence Minister Krishna Menon took a ride in it.

Impressed, he ordered that a more powerful version be made.

The project, however, was shelved when Menon fell from favour and resigned after the debacle of the

Indian Army against the Chinese in 1962. But one day, ADE Director O.P. Mediratta ordered Kalam to dust off the hovercraft for a demonstration for an important visitor. The visitor duly came, flew in the hovercraft and left impressed. He was Dr M.G.K. Menon of the Tata Institute of Fundamental Research (TIFR).

A week later, thanks to Menon, Kalam got a call to

India's first space research centre was in this church at Thumba, which was handed over by the Christian Community

come for an interview for the post of Rocket Engineer by the Indian Committee for Space Research (INCOSPAR). This had been set up recently to spearhead India's space efforts. The interview took place in Bombay, with the questions being asked mainly by Dr Vikram Sarabhai. It became clear that Sarabhai was not so much interested in the extent of Kalam's knowledge base, as

Testing the hovercraft

in his ability to think. Kalam was selected and sent for training to the TIFR computer centre. From there, he went to Thumba, in Kerala, where an Equatorial Rocket Launching Station was set up in 1962.

Almost immediately, Kalam was sent by Sarabhai for a six-month training course at the National Aeronautics and Space Administration (NASA) centre in the US. It was his first trip abroad. After a brief visit to Rameswaram, where he had an emotional meeting with his family, Kalam arrived at NASA's Langley Research Centre in Virginia, and then went to the Goddard Space Flight Centre.

On a visit to the Flight Facility at Wallops Island, he happened to see a painting in the lobby depicting a battle scene in which rockets were being fired. It turned out to be a picture of Tipu Sultan's troops attacking the British with rockets! Buoyed by the discovery of this unexpected and to him, unknown, chapter in the history of rocketry, Kalam vowed that he would devote himself to resurrecting the science of rocketry in India.

An unhappy fallout of the US visit took place almost 40 years later, when, following the rapid developments in India's missile programme, it was said that they were the result of what Kalam had learned at NASA. A caustic Kalam remarked that the only rocket he had seen take off had failed in its mission. After launch, it had landed on the jeep belonging to NASA's director! He saw it as another indication of the inability of the West to appreciate India's expertise, and an attempt to strangle her scientific skills.

Kalam returned home in time to witness the first rocket launch in India on 21 November 1963. It was a NASA-made Nike-Apache. Kalam and his colleagues manually placed the rocket on the launch pad, after the hydraulic lift failed just before launch time, and a disaster was averted. Following the successful launch, Sarabhai developed ambitious plans for an Indian Satellite Launch Vehicle (ISLV). Different people were given different tasks to do, and Kalam was asked to hone his expertise on a Rocket-Assisted Take-Off System (RATO), which was normally used for sending up weather rockets. Kalam had to work with scientists from the US, USSR,

A voluble Kalam makes a point to a smiling Vikram Sarabbai

and France, who were giving assistance to India's space programme.

For Kalam and his young colleagues, these were heady days. Sarabhai had given them his full confidence, and was willing to try out all of their ideas. He, seemingly, knew when an idea was going to bear fruit and when it was necessary to discard before going too far with it. If there was a failure, he would still find something good to say about it, and look at the bright side. When his team was at the drawing board stage, he would bring in a foreign engineer, forcing them to stretch their abilities and come up with a solution. From Sarabhai, Kalam learned not only the science of rocketry, but also leadership by trust.

Kalam explains SLV-3 results to Prime Minister Indira Gandhi as his colleagues look on

The rocket programme really took off with the launch of Rohini-75, the first indigenous rocket, in November 1967. In 1969, Kalam was summoned to Delhi by Sarabhai and asked if a RATO system for launching fighter aircrafts in the Himalayas could be developed within 18 months. He said that it was feasible and was immediately put in charge of the project, which was successfully completed. A second development took place when Kalam became a member of a Missile Panel in the Ministry of Defence, charged with the task of indigenising all the parts required for a missile, which had to be imported at the time.

Kalam was then put in charge of the team which was to develop the fourth stage for the SLV under the Indian

SLV-3 on the launch pad

Space Research Organisation (ISRO). In December 1971, he received a personal blow when Dr Sarabhai suddenly died. But work had to go on in the absence of the master and it did. The RATO system was perfected and made operational by 1972. Kalam's role in the SLV programme also underwent a change – he became the project manager for SLV-3. His job was to coordinate the work of all the different teams. The first attempt to launch on 10 March 1979 was a failure, but the second attempt on 18 July 1980 was successful.

Kalam had a memorable meeting with Wernher Von Braun, the legendary rocket scientist who had designed the VI and V2 rockets which devastated

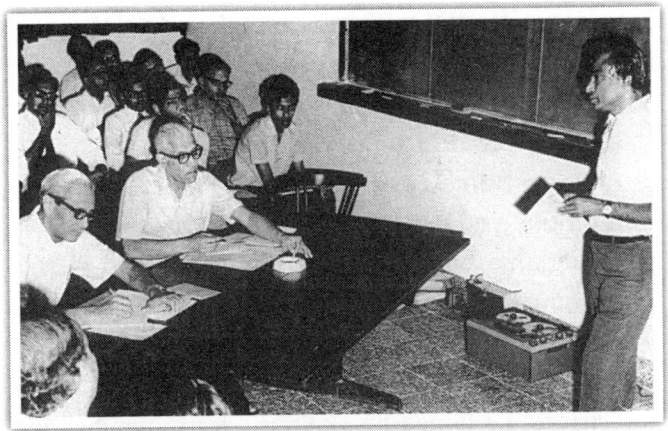

Kalam addresses a review meeting on SLV-3

London in World War II, when the latter came on a visit to Thumba. Von Braun told Kalam, 'You may be having your own troubles, but you should remember that we don't build on just successes, we also build on failures.'

Simultaneously, Kalam became involved in the efforts of the Defence Research and Development Organisation (DRDO) to build surface-to-air missiles. A result was the creation of the Defence Research Development

Wernher Von Braun working on one of his rocket engines

Laboratory (DRDL). Kalam shifted to DRDL as its director in 1982 through the efforts of the scientific advisor to the Defence Minister, Dr Raja Ramanna, the scientist involved in India's nuclear programme.

Fate had plucked Kalam out of nowhere and put him on the road to success. Attempts have been made to dismiss his contributions to the rocket and missile programmes, by pointing to the fact that he was part of a team, and that his work was largely managerial. Kalam was definitely part of a team, and a manager – given the chance; he honed his skills as a team member and a manager. All his colleagues attest to the fact that he was an inveterate problem solver, whether it involved a difficulty of an engineering nature or otherwise. These skills were to be tested in the next stage of his life.

Chapter 3
The Mission of Self-Reliance

To succeed in your mission, you must have single-minded devotion to your goal

— *A. P. J. Abdul Kalam*

Kalam had till now been engaged in designing and building rockets. The shift from ISRO to DRDL was more than just a shift from one organisation to another – it was a shift from rocketry to missiles, from the civilian to the military arena. Kalam's military philosophy is very simple – India must have the necessary weapons not just to stop any aggressor, but to avert such an eventuality.

The first task that Kalam set was that of devising a clear and well-defined programme for developing indigenous missiles. A committee under Kalam put up a ₹ 390-crore proposal, spread over 12 years, to develop two types of missiles – a low-level quick reaction Tactical Core Vehicle and a medium-range surface-to-surface weapon system. It was proposed that a surface-to-air medium-range weapon system, capable of multiple-targetting, be developed in the second phase. Another proposal was for a third-generation anti-tank missile, and a Re-entry Experimental Launch Vehicle (REX). The proposals were given to Defence Minister R. Venkataraman, and cleared by the Union Cabinet.

The plans for the Integrated Guide Missile System Programme (IGDMP) were further developed after approval was received. The focus was to develop

One of DRDO's rocket trials

self-reliance in this field. The surface-to-surface weapon system was named Prithvi, the Tactical Core Vehicle was Trishul, the surface-to-air system was Akash, the anti-tank project was Nag, and the REX was to be Agni.

Kalam was so involved in the formulation of the plans for the missile programme that he forgot that sister Zohara's daughter, Zammela, was about to be married. There was no way that he would be able to get home in time as the wedding was that very evening. The news was conveyed to Venkataraman, who immediately arranged for Kalam to leave for Chennai on the Indian Airlines flight in an hour's time. There, an Indian Air Force helicopter was waiting to take him home. Much to his relief, Kalam did not fail the family that had stood by him always.

Agni tower over its creator

Missiles at the Republic Day parade

The IGDMP Project called for over 400 scientists to participate in it, with five project directors who would, in turn, train another 25 project directors and team leaders for the future. It was Kalam's job to lead and co-ordinate the work of these talented people, and solve problems that may arise. 26 June 1984 saw the flight test of the Inertial Guidance System and the Devil missile was tested. The first launch of Trishul took place on 16 September 1985, under the IGDMP.

A setback of sorts occurred when the launch of the Agni missile had to be aborted on 20 April 1989, due to the malfunctioning of some instruments. The same problem arose on 1 May and the launch was again scrapped. There was much derision in the media at

Jubilant colleagues carry Kalam on their shoulders after Agni took off

the repeated failures, but Kalam remained unperturbed. Finally, Agni was launched on 22 May. Prime Minister Rajiv Gandhi's assessment in a message to Kalam was correct: '…a major achievement… Agni is a reflection of our commitment to the indigenous development of advanced technologies to the nation's defence.'

The story goes that the day before the launch was to take place, Defence Minister K.C. Pant asked Kalam how he would like to celebrate the success of Agni. Kalam immediately said that he wanted one lakh saplings to be planted at the Research Centre Imarat. His wish was fulfilled, and the area is today lush with greenery.

For his role, Kalam was given the Padma Vibhushan on Republic Day in 1990, following the Padma Bhushan of 1981. The other scientists on the project were also honoured with the Padma Shri. The next year, Trishul was also launched successfully, completing the first stage of the missile programme.

Receiving the Padma Bhushan from President Neelam Sanjeeva Reddy

On the verge of retirement, Kalam still had another major role to play. The victory of the Bharatiya Janata Party-led National Democratic Alliance in 1998 brought to power a government committed to the exercise of the nuclear option. In 1996, the short-lived BJP Government had given the green light for a nuclear test, but its fall ended that experiment. This time around, there was no looking back.

Prime Minister Atal Bihari Vajpayee ordered that nuclear tests be carried out at Pokhran in Rajasthan, where India had exploded a nuclear device in 1974. Kalam's task was that of coordinating the work of all the numerous agencies involved in the secret operation – the

Kalam with Vajpayee and Defence Minister George Fernandes at Pokhran after the nuclear tests

Army, the Defence establishment, the DRDO etc. Kalam was a cog in the wheel, a major one for Pokhran-II, and not the prime mover, as many have been led to believe. Nevertheless, his role as the public face of the bomb was formed when he addressed the press following the tests. Interestingly, everybody involved in Pokhran-II had an alias. Kalam was, ironically, General Prithviraj!

Kalam also spent time over a report for the Planning Commission on 'India As a Knowledge Superpower.' It focussed on the possibilities inherent in Information Technology. He also worked on *Vision 2020,* a blueprint

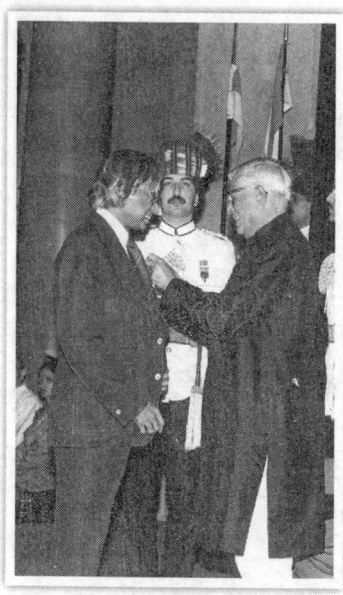

Receiving the Padma Vibbushan from President R. Venkataraman, 1990

for the regeneration of India, which we will discuss later.

In November 1999, Kalam was appointed the Principal Scientific Advisor to the Government. He quit in November 2001, as he wanted to devote time to his other projects and charities. He was also believed to be unhappy at the lack of executive powers which went with the job. He especially wanted to meet at least one lakh schoolchildren, and share his dream of India with them. He joined the faculty of Anna University at Chennai as Professor of Technology and Societal Transformation, which became his base. He began to criss-cross the country, and by mid-2002, had met at least 60,000 children. On one of these occasions, he had a narrow escape when his helicopter crashlanded in Jharkhand.

As so often in his life, just when he thought that he was free to pursue his own interests, fate took a hand

Receiving the Bharat Ratna from President K. R. Narayanan

again, and steered him back to Delhi, which he had left less than a year earlier. But things were different this time. He was now the President of India.

Chapter 4
The Unexpected President

Great dreams of great dreamers are always transcended
— *A. P. J. Abdul Kalam*

On 25 July 2002, the installation of the 11th President of India took place in the Central Hall of Parliament. It was Abdul Kalam who took the Oath of Office. How did a man who had left the government to pursue his passionate dreams end up in the highest office in the land? The answer lies both in the dynamics

Presidential candidate Dr A.P.J. Abdul Kalam files his nomination papers for the presidential election in the presence of Prime Minister Atal Bihari Vajpayee, Leader of the Opposition Sonia Gandhi and a galaxy of political leaders, on 18 June 2002

of the political environment of India, as well as in the personality of Kalam himself.

Since the fall of the Congress Party in the 1996 elections, coalition governments had governed India. The National Democratic Alliance (NDA), comprising the Bharatiya Janata Party and a number of other national and regional outfits, was in power, under the premiership of Atal Bihari Vajpayee. Though the NDA controlled the Centre and governments in a number of states, the non-NDA parties controlled most of them, with the Congress Party in the saddle in key regions.

The members of Parliament and the members of all state assemblies elect the President of India. The margin between the NDA and the opposition in the Electoral College was very narrow. Therefore, it was necessary to swing the Congress behind a suitable candidate. The candidature of the Maharashtra Governor RC. Alexander, a former aide to Prime Ministers Indira Gandhi and Rajiv Gandhi, was proposed by the NDA. It met unexpected resistance from the Telegu Desam, a key supporter of the government. It wanted Vice-President Krishan Kant elevated to the Presidency. The Congress also opposed Alexander. The Congress and the Left parties were, at the same time, trying to persuade President K.R. Narayanan to stand for a second term. He, however, made it clear that he was averse to a contest and would agree to stand only as a consensus candidate.

The NDA withdrew Alexander's name from contention and Vajpayee announced on 10 June 2002 that Abdul Kalam would be their candidate. The suggestion had been made by Trinamool Congress leader Mamata Banerjee, and it was seized upon as a way out of the morass. The Congress, Samajwadi Party and others, who would have otherwise opposed the NDA, immediately fell in line. A reason given for their support of Kalam was that, at one level, they did not wish to be seen as opposing a Muslim candidate. But more than that, Kalam was a known quantity to them, and much respected for his abilities and personality.

Prime Minister Vajpayee meets Dr Abdul Kalam in New Delhi on 17 June 2002

The Left parties, however, opposed Kalam on the grounds that he was unqualified for the office. Further, they said that their candidate would be the legendary freedom fighter, 87-year-old Captain Lakshmi Sehgal, of the Indian National Army.

At this juncture, it was necessary to consider the question of whether Kalam was competent to hold the Office of the President. The opposition of the Left was woven around the premise that since political conditions in the country dictated that there could not be single-party governments, and coalitions would be the norm, it was necessary for any president to be conversant with the Constitution and constitutional law. The Left also said that it was necessary for there to be a president other than one from the NDA, given the communal situation in the country.

This, of course, completely overlooked the fact that in any given situation, where there was a crisis or any ambiguity, the president could approach constitutional experts, the Supreme Court, his predecessors, and examine precedents, if any – as even presidents well-versed in constitutional law would. Kalam, too, could do the same. Moreover, if this were to disqualify Kalam, then, if the same criterion were to be applied to Sehgal, she too would have failed the test. As far as the communal question was concerned, the very fact that the NDA had opted for a Muslim could be a signal, however symbolic, to the minorities.

The stand of the Left was further undermined when Sehgal, campaigning across the country, declared that she saw Vajpayee as an enemy, and went on to say that she saw Kalam as the embodiment of the nuclear bomb. Kalam, to his credit, quietly ignored these barbs.

When Union Minister for Parliamentary Affairs, Pramod Mahajan, asked him when he would like to file his nomination papers, the answer was short and succinct – 'Anytime' – a departure from the tradition of doing something at an astrologically auspicious moment. Kalam filed his papers on 18 June 2002 in the presence of the prime minister. He paid the ₹

15,000 deposit from his own pocket. Kalam then issued a letter addressed to all electors, which, for the first time, gave a coherent, complete, and concise account of his views across the entire gamut of political, social and economic issues, which we will discuss in detail later. The election, of course, was a foregone conclusion and Kalam took almost 90 per cent of the vote – only Dr S. Radhakrishnan and K.R. Narayanan had earlier touched this figure. He thanked those who had voted for him, saying, 'It's a great day when a poor man's son can become president.'

There were several firsts in the inaugural ceremony of the new president. It was for the first time that the inauguration took place in Parliament House rather than Rashtrapati Bhavan. It was the first time that the president gave an address immediately after being sworn in. It was also the first time that a president quoted poetry. It was yet another first that a blueprint for development was spelled out; and it was the first time a president did not mention Mahatma Gandhi – though the speech itself was Gandhian in spirit.

Kalam continued his informal ways. His first visits to Rajghat and Shantivan, the memorials of Gandhi and Nehru, were low-key, in tune with the man himself. And the first signs of an independent president came when Kalam wanted to address parliamentarians on development. This, however, was scrapped after the

Dr A.P.J. Abdul Kalam delivering his speech on his assumption of office as the President of India in the Central Hall of Parliament in New Delhi on 25 July 2002, as out-going President K.R. Narayanan, Vice President Kant and Lok Sabba Speaker Manohar Joshi listen

government asked to see his speech first. Nevertheless, a similar meet with freedom fighters took place. A year later, he did manage to address members of Parliament on his vision of India at Rashtrapati Bhavan. Again, he electrified the country with the announcement that he would visit riot-torn Gujarat to study relief – never before had a president consciously stepped into such a political minefield.

How would Kalam acquit himself as president? It was, of course, too early to make any predictions. However, one could discern certain trends emerging.

Kalam was not allowing himself to be confined within the four imposing walls of the Rashtrapati Bhavan, quietly signing papers. He was continuing his contacts with the people in any way that he could, avoiding the pitfall of isolation. Kalam fully realised the potential inherent in using the presidency as a 'bully pulpit', in US President Teddy Roosevelt's memorable phrase. He was using the power of his office to focus attention on urgent issues of the day, and hammering away at his vision of a developed India. He would not blot his copybook, but he was not a copybook president – Kalam proved to be a creative president.

Chapter 5
The Man And His Vision

The ignited mind is the most powerful resource on earth
— *A. P. J. Abdul Kalam*

The position that Abdul Kalam has achieved in national life is due entirely to the kind of person he is; and his exceptional vision of what India not only can be, but, in his eyes, also must be. The two cannot be separated; they are inextricably one.

Kalam is a man of few needs. A bachelor – he escaped marriage when his sister-in-law and niece fell ill – he eats a simple vegetarian meal and leads such a spartan life that he became known as Kalam Iyer. Life must have been very difficult for the cooks at Rashtrapati Bhavan! He recites the Holy Quran and the Bhagavadgita everyday. He greatly admires the Tamil classic *Thirukkural* by Thiruvalluvar, whose influence is apparent – he quoted at length from it in his inaugural address. Kalam is an accomplished poet in Tamil, and in his MIT days, won a literary prize for a Tamil essay on *Let Us Build Our Own Aircraft*. He is also an amateur player of the veena, and professes *Sri Raga* to be his favourite piece of music.

He is also extremely modest. Whenever a project was successful, he discounted his own role, and attributed it all to the efforts of his team. He has no airs or sense of self-importance about him, and is accessible to all and sundry. His generosity is legendary. Colleagues recall how he would quietly distribute food and fruits, which was given to him, among his drivers.

Kalam has an extraordinary feel for, and rapport with, children. A former colleague, Anand Parthasarthy has this story to tell from the time when Prithvi was to be launched. The deputy project leader for Prithvi, V.K. Saraswat, had given a schoolgirl in Secunderabad details about the missile's size and shape, which she used to make a papier mache model. A photograph was published in a newspaper. Kalam suggested that since the girl had done such a good job, she must be invited to Hyderabad. She was duly brought in a staff car, given a tour of the laboratory, shown the actual Prithvi, and had lunch with the scientists. In the end, she met Kalam, who swept his work aside to sit down and talk to her, asking about her hobbies, school etc.

During the Gujarat riots, Kalam met a schoolgirl in Anand, and asked her what India's biggest enemy was. Such is Kalam's ability to reach out to children and get them to talk because he takes them seriously, that she immediately answered: 'poverty.' Perhaps his most important meeting with the next generation was with a 14-year-old girl in Hyderabad, who asked him for an autograph. Kalam asked her what her goal in life was. She replied, 'I want to live in a developed India.' This is the vision that Kalam has always promoted.

Kalam has also been engaged in the activities of the Society For Biomedical Technology, which brought together several government departments, medical institutes and defence laboratories. The idea is to develop indigenous medical technologies. One result is the Kalam-Raju Stent, which was developed by defence labs and Dr B. Soma Raju of Hyderabad. The stent, which is used as a scaffolding to dilate constricted arteries after a heart attack, costs ₹ 25,000 against ₹ 60,000 for an imported one.

An issue which saddens Kalam is the negative and obstructionist attitudes of superiors. He notes: 'What makes life in Indian organisations difficult is the widespread prevalence of contemptuous pride. It stops us from listening to our juniors, subordinates and people down the line. You cannot expect a person to deliver results if you humiliate him, nor can you expect him to be creative if you abuse him or despise him. The line between firmness and harshness, between strong leadership and bullying, between discipline and vindictiveness is very fine, but it has to be drawn.'

What drives him? The answer may lie in the response that he gave to a student who wished to be a nuclear scientist, and wanted his advice on how to go about it. The answer was: 'Dream, dream, dream. Think, think, think. And then put that into action, action, action. OK?' This, obviously, is an observation from experience.

But remember, Kalam has also known poverty. In the section on *Thoughts* on his website, there is the following meditation: 'I will not be presumptuous enough to say that my life can be a role model for anybody; but some poor child living in an obscure place, in an underprivileged social setting, may find a little solace in the way my destiny has been shaped. It could, perhaps, help such children liberate themselves from the bondage of their illusionary backwardness and

With close colleague Y.S. Rajan (left) and Y.S. Nayar

hopelessness.' Again, in his memoirs he notes: 'The biggest problem Indian youth faced, I felt, was a lack of vision, a lack of direction...What I wanted to say was that no one, however poor, underprivileged or small need feel disheartened by life.'

This is the driving force, the burning passion, which fuels the vision of Abdul Kalam.

But what, exactly, is this vision? It is a vision of an India harnessing technology and the creative powers of her people to realise its rightful place in the world, and lifting her people from the poverty and sloth in which they are mired.

What are the aims of this mission? They are threefold: India has to become economically and commercially powerful, commensurate with the size of the country; self-reliance in defence needs for equipment and weapons; and India should take her rightful place in the world.

And how was this to be achieved? Through *Technology Vision 2020,* which consists of 17 technology packages. This was developed by 500 experts over a period of two years for the Technology Information, Forecasting and Assessment Council. These packages are linked to five areas where India has core competence. Integrated action has to take place for the mission to be achieved. Kalam has listed the following areas: agriculture and food processing, reliable and quality electric power for all parts of the country, education, healthcare, and information technology.

In his letter to parliamentarians, Kalam spelled out his political views clearly for the first time (See *The Election Manifesto).* There is nothing in them to cause any surprise. He believes in the sanctity of the basic structure of the Constitution, secularism, harmonious Centre-State relations, and empowerment of women. There are, however, two aspects which bear notice. Firstly, he emphasises the primacy of national security – not surprising, given his background; secondly, he focuses on the environment, social justice, India as a Knowledge Society, with a fierce reiteration of his belief that children are the future, and need to be given good education, healthcare etc., to realise their

Abdul Kalam talking to children

potential. In short, we have a manifesto which espouses not a single-issue, but a rainbow vision, as it were. It envisions national security and welfare issues as being linked together, and not as separate entities.

Kalam's vision of India is that of an empowered nation.

Envoi

President Kalam entered the Rashtrapati Bhavan at an age when most people play out time into the twilight. Rising from the most humble of households, sheer determination and hard work have been the hallmark of a lifetime spent in the service of the nation. The lessons learnt in life made him even more determined to share his vision of a Developed India, second to none, with others, and recruit them into this mission, and make it a reality. Dr Kalam's journey is not over yet.

The Election Manifesto

The text of a letter sent by Dr Kalam to all Members of Parliament.

Dear Honourable Member of Parliament,

My greetings to you, for your happiness and well-being.

As you are aware, I am contesting as a candidate for the election of the 11th President of India, with the support of many political parties, eminent leaders, and a broad cross-section of our people. I am truly overwhelmed at the wholehearted endorsement I have received from a wide spectrum of the country's political establishment, cutting across the divide between the ruling and most of the opposition parties. I take this to be a symbol of the essential unity of our political establishment, which transcends its proud diversity in matters of national importance. This is a good portent for our democracy.

I am, indeed, grateful to all those who have supported me for giving me this opportunity, which will enable me to work with you to realize our shared dream of transforming India into a strong, prosperous, peaceful, resurgent and humane nation playing its rightful role in the benign transformation of the affairs of the world. I also express my sincerest thanks to the people of this great nation, from whom I have received an enthusiastic outpouring of letters and e-mails in the past few weeks. In addition, the flood of messages sent to me by Indians residing abroad amplifies their sentiment. I am touched by the comments in the print and electronic media echoing the decision of the mainstream of India's political establishment to support my candidature. I have also been enriched by their different suggestions and ideas.

Friends, the people of India, as well as all of you in the Electoral College, know me to be a person with simple origins and who has served his country in his own humble way. It speaks for the power and vitality of India's democracy that a poor boy from a small island in Tamil Nadu can travel this far in the service of his Motherland and now be considered for the responsibilities of Rashtrapati Bhavan.

Legendary personalities like Dr Rajendra Prasad, Dr S. Radhakrishnan and Dr Zakir Husain have occupied it in the past. If I have offered myself as a candidate for the highest Constitutional office in the country, it is entirely because of your trust and faith in me. Hence, the first pledge I would like to take is to remain true to your trust, and, if elected, to always remain unwaveringly faithful to the letter and spirit of the Constitution in performing my duty.

Permit me to take this opportunity to briefly outline my vision for the Presidency.

Basic Structure Of The Constitution Unalterable

We are truly blessed that the makers of our Constitution, under the farsighted and scholarly leadership of Dr Babasaheb Ambedkar, have bequeathed to us one of the most enlightened statutes in the world. Parliamentary democracy is the core of our governance system, with the President as the Head of State and the overall custodian of the Constitution. There is an excellent balance between the Legislature, Executive and Judiciary with proper checks and safeguards. The basic structure of our Constitution has stood the test of time and shown itself to be having the vigour, vitality and eternal freshness that make it capable of meeting any challenge that new circumstances might hurl at it. At the same time, our Constitution is also innately resilient so as to be responsive to the demands of changing situations. I am sure all of you will agree that we need to zealously preserve this principle of 'change with continuity', which is indeed the signature tune of India's millennia-old civilization. Thus, my first and foremost task is to respect the Constitutional process, in the best interests of our people and the nation, as provided for in the Constitution without fear or favour and with fairness and firmness.

Harmonious Centre-State Relations

The second principle that I shall fervently uphold is the harmonious relations between the Centre and the States. India is a Union of States, based on the framework of cooperative federalism. I stand for a strong Centre and strong States. I also share the near consensual belief that the time has come to devolve more power to the States, since decentralization is the key to faster and more balanced development. At the same time, we should also move quickly to empower our Panchayati Raj institutions both financially and administratively, if necessary through relevant changes to the existing systems. Mahatma Gandhi's exhortation that India lives in her villages rings true even today and would be so in the future too.

Social And Economic Justice

An inescapable imperative of development in the Indian context is to ensure that the fruits of economic growth and social progress reach the deprived sections of our population. Scheduled Castes, Scheduled Tribes, OBCs, including those belonging to minority communities, constitute a large section of our society. India cannot become strong and developed if they continue to remain weak and underdeveloped. Therefore, our strategy for removal of poverty must be multi-dimensional with a strong focus on Social Justice. It should be centred around a sound programme for the removal of regional and social imbalances. One thrust area could be integrated rural development, with promotion of agriculture, agro-industries and cottage industries as its engine and multiple connectivities—physical, digital and marketing—as its propellant.

Women's Empowerment

Gender Justice, sadly, has still remained a neglected aspect of Social Justice. Indian women are the custodians of cultural and family values. If properly empowered, they can contribute immensely to our nation's all-round development much more effectively. I would, therefore, like to see that proper systems and mechanisms are in place to enable increased participation of women in our

Parliament, State Legislatures and other political and public bodies. Simultaneously, both the Government and society should work together to expand the opportunities for women's education and for putting an end to all types of atrocities and injustices committed against them. I would like to see India to be a role model for the rest of the world in this crucial aspect.

Primacy Of National Security

Along with speedy development aimed at elimination of poverty and unemployment, national security has to be recognized by every Indian as a priority. Indeed, making India strong and self-reliant—economically, socially and militarily—is our foremost duty towards our motherland. We owe it to ourselves and to the future generations. I have said this before, but it bears reiteration, that, India, which has suffered invasions for many centuries in the past, must be in a position to defend herself against all and any odds. I am proud of my role in our country's space, nuclear and missile programmes, because I believe that these have greatly strengthened India's national security, enabled us to follow an independent foreign policy, and helped us to overcome challenges created by technology denial and economic sanctions by powerful countries.

These S&T programmes, most of which have developmental spin-offs, have enhanced our national pride by putting India in the category of technologically advanced nations. Our national security strategy is guided purely by defensive considerations. It poses no threat to any country in the world.

Foreign Policy

India's foreign policy has always stood on a strong edifice of national consensus. Together with you, I wish to develop and further strengthen our ties of friendship and mutually beneficial cooperation with all countries in the world.

J&K, An Inalienable Part Of India

I share the nation's concern and outrage at cross-border terrorism, which our neighbour has pursued as a matter of state policy. This policy, aimed at destabilization and dismemberment of India, is doomed. Jammu & Kashmir was, is, and shall remain an inseparable part of India. From Kashmir to Kanyakumari, from Kutch to Kohima, and from Lakshwadeep to Andaman-Nicobar Islands, we are one indivisible people, and one unbreakable nation, unified by the golden thread of our culture and civilization and our common vision of a peaceful, democratic and modern India.

Secularism, The Essence Of Indianness

Here I also wish to reiterate my unflinching commitment to the principle of secularism, which is the cornerstone of our nationhood. Intolerance and violence in the name of religion is the worst form of irreligion. True religion is the Ocean of Spiritualism in which all faiths shine in brilliance. To people in politics and government, it teaches the message of leadership with compassion and fairness. A unique source of my pride in being an Indian, since my school days, is that our country is home to all the world's religions and has always propounded and practiced the truth of *Sarva Dharma Samabhav* (equal respect for all religions). India is a plural society, with equal rights and responsibilities for citizens belonging to people of all religions, regions, castes, classes and linguistic communities. The broad and enthusiastic support I have received from all corners and communities of India is itself a resounding reminder that our secular ethos is alive and vibrant.

Unity Of Minds

We are a country with rich diversity. We have developed a democratic polity under the framework of our Republican Constitution. These are our strengths. It is but natural that there are, and there will be, differences in viewpoints and perceptions on certain issues. Opportunity to express differing opinions and finding solutions through dialogue and due processes of the rule of law, are important elements of the functioning of democratic systems. It is also a fact that there are a few unresolved issues that trouble us occasionally and a few additional problems, sometimes painful, get added to our system. I would like to sincerely endeavour to work for bringing about unity of minds while fully respecting and maintaining the rich pluralistic traditions of our country.

Natural Resources And The Environment

Economic development and related actions are important and crucial. But it is also necessary to protect nature's endowments available to our country. Conserving, sustaining and enriching our natural resources, including the environment, are extremely important for the well-being of not only the present but also our future generations. In fact, it is our ethical responsibility towards the whole globe.

Finer Aspects Of Human Life—Arts, Literature, Sports, etc.

While economic, political, international, legal, scientific, technological and many other professional tasks, including national security, are vital for the nation, its soul also expresses itself through literature, music and arts, culture, crafts, religious and spiritual philosophies, sports as well as other finer aspects of human life. The diversity of languages, traditions and religions in our country adds a unique dimension to this precious national heritage. Throughout my life, I have enjoyed many facets of this heritage and been a connoisseur of some. I would like to actively encourage the growth of aesthetics in all areas of our national life. I would like to explore possibilities of using modern technologies and systems to make our people, as also the people of the world, more aware of the richness and diversity of India's heritage. I would also like to emphasise probity and commitment to values in public life, including in polity.

Young People, Our Unique Strength

Although we are an ancient nation, India is a young country, demographically speaking. We have a large, and growing, percentage of young people in our society. It is a great strength today and is going to be so for decades to come. Therefore, we all need to cherish and encourage our young people, irrespective of where they are born and what they are doing. We all should dedicate ourselves to provide our young people all the opportunities: first of all good nourishment, good healthcare, sanitation and sound education that combines development of knowledge, skills and values and thus enables them to become useful citizens and prosper in a competitive world. We should pay greater attention to promote sports, the spirit of adventure, exploration and innovation, and their natural aptitude for idealism and voluntary social work. We should rekindle a strong sense of nationalism in them, manifesting itself in better work culture and readiness for self-sacrifice for achieving larger societal goals. We should devise effective governmental and non-governmental mechanism to make this happen so that our youth can develop as responsible and capable citizens of tomorrow. Our young men and women are the greatest asset of our country. I will commit myself to encourage every action that can make this dream a reality very soon.

India As A Knowledge Superpower

Friends, science, technology and their applications have been my main calling in life so far. Accordingly, my vision for the future of India is strongly rooted in my faith in the power of scientific and technological knowledge and their beneficial applications. Our greatest and most precious national resource is our one billion people, who have inherited a priceless intellectual, cultural, artistic and artisanal heritage. But how can their minds be ignited? How can their talents, skills and knowledge be rendered more productive, and more rewarding to them so that they become active agents of a society-wide transformation in education, healthcare, agriculture, industry, and services; so that we will witness large-scale employment generation, high productivity, rural prosperity and urban renewal; so that our national security becomes impregnable; so that we achieve greater societal harmony and peace; so that we vastly expand the scope of e-governance, which is crucial even from the point of view of making our democracy perform and deliver better?

I share the conviction of our political leaders and others as enshrined in the Scientific Policy Resolution, and reiterated many times by our own academic and R&D establishment, that the answer lies, chiefly, in making India a science- and technology-driven nation. We have already demonstrated our core competence in agriculture, Information Technology, space research, atomic energy, defence, some aspects of healthcare and select areas of manufacturing and services, and have started to reap its benefits. We should now develop similar core competence in some critical technologies to address our national priorities. We should aim to become a Knowledge Superpower within this decade, so that India can face the challenges of growing competition in the years of globalisation and our hard-earned freedom is reliably nurtured.

If I get an opportunity, we will work together, within the Parliamentary system, to generate a road map for transforming India from a 'Developing Nation' into a 'Developed Nation'. In my book *India 2020: A Vision For The New Millennium,* I have said, 'A developed India by 2020, or even earlier, is not a dream. It need not even be a mere vision in the minds of many Indians. It is a mission we can all take up—and succeed.'

Youth And Children, The Source Of Our Hope

You might ask me: 'What is the source of your optimism?' My answer will be: 'India's youth and India's children.'

In the past twelve months, I have interacted with over 55,000 school children from most of the States of our country. They are all dreaming to live in a prosperous India, with peace and harmony, and looking for role models for exemplary leadership in every field and also looking for opportunities for themselves to contribute. When I look into their eyes, when I listen to them speak, I am awestruck by the heavy responsibility that rests on the shoulders of elders like us. Together with you, I want to work to fulfill their dreams—to fulfill our dreams. O Almighty! Empower my mind to always think and act that my nation is bigger than me.

May I, therefore, appeal to you to cast your valuable vote to elect me to serve this great Nation as its next President and work towards the fulfillment of our commonly cherished vision of India as a Developed Nation.

Jai Hind!
Yours sincerely

अब्दुल कलाम

Dr Kalam in full flow at one of his lectures

The Vision of India

The text of the Inaugural Speech delivered by Dr Abdul Kalam on his assumption of the office of the President of India on 25 July 2002 at the Central Hall of the Parliament of India, at New Delhi.

Respected Shri Narayananji, Mr Vice-President, Mr Prime Minister, Mr Deputy Prime Minister, Chief Justice of India, Speaker of Lok Sabha, Members of the Union Council of Ministers, Governors, Chief Ministers, Deputy Chairperson of Rajya Sabha, Deputy Speaker of Lok Sabha, Members of Parliament, Excellencies, friends and children—my greetings to all of you. When I see in front of me, the distinguished dignitaries including a number of senior diplomats representing their countries and other eminent personalities, a beautiful Thiagarajaswamigal's Keerthana in Sri Raga echoes from my heart—*Endrao Mahaanubbavalu andbariggi vandanamulu* which means, 'I salute all the great nobler hearted human beings'.

I thank the Members of Parliament and State Legislatures for having elected me. The endorsement I have received from the nation, giving me the responsibility to realize our shared dream of India with prosperity, harmony and strength is really overwhelming. Ten illustrious personages have adorned this office of the President and contributed to the nation building with their outstanding personal qualities. I salute them all. While I assume the office of the President of Republic of India with humility and gratefully recognizing the immense trust the people of the country and the political system have reposed in me, I promise to endeavour to fulfill the aspirations of our people.

Indian civilizational heritage is built on universal spirit. India always stood for friendship and extends warm hands to the whole world.

We have made significant achievements in the last fifty years in food production, health sector, higher education, media and mass communication, industrial infrastructure, information technology, science and technology and defence. Our nation is endowed with natural resources, vibrant people and traditional value system. In spite of these resources, a number of our people are below the poverty line, undernourished, and lack primary education itself. Our aim is to empower them to be poverty-free, healthy and literate. A country needs to have the characteristics as defined in *Thirukkural,* composed over 2000 years ago:

> *Pini inmai Selvam Vilaivinbam Emam.*
> *Aniyenba Nattirkiv vainthu*

That is, 'the important elements that constitute a nation are: being disease free; high productivity; harmonious living and strong defence.' All our efforts should be focused towards building these five elements in a coherent and in an integrated manner. I am convinced that our nation with a strong, vibrant and billion-plus population can contribute to realize these elements.

Today our country is facing challenges such as cross-border terrorism, certain internal conflicts and unemployment. To face these challenges, there must be a vision to ensure focused action of one billion citizens of this great country with varied capabilities. What can be that vision? It can be none other than transforming India into a 'Developed Nation'. Can government alone achieve this vision? Now, we need a movement in the country. This is the time to ignite the minds of the people for this movement. We will work for it. We cannot emerge as a developed nation if we do not learn to transact with speed. I recall the saintly poet Kabir's wisdom to us:

Kaal Kare So Aaj Kar
Aaj Kare So Ab

that means, 'What you want to do tomorrow do it today, and what you want to do today do it now.'

This vision of developed nation needs to be achieved with Parliamentary democracy, which is the core of our governance system. The basic structure of our Constitution has stood the test of time. I am confident that it will continue to be responsive to the demands of changing situations. The first and foremost task is to respect and uphold the constitutional processes, in the best interest of our people and our nation, without fear or favour and with fairness and firmness. India is a Union of States based on the framework of cooperative federalism. Within the co-operative framework, there is also a requirement to develop competitive strengths for the States so that they can excel at the national level and the global level. Competitiveness helps in ensuring economic and managerial efficiency and to be creative to meet new challenges. These are essential to survive and prosper in a fast-changing world of today. In addition, in order to strengthen democratic processes and institutions, we should all truly strive for substantive decentralization.

I wish to emphasize my unflinching commitment to the principle of secularism, which is the cornerstone of our nationhood and which is the key feature of our civilizational strength. During the last one year I met a number of spiritual leaders of all religions. They all echoed one message, that is, unity of minds and hearts of our people will happen and we will see the golden age of our country, very soon. I would like to endeavour to work for bringing about unity of minds among the divergent traditions of our country.

Along with speedy development aimed at elimination of poverty and unemployment, national security has to be recognised by every Indian as a national priority. Indeed, making India strong and self-reliant—economically, socially, and militarily—is our foremost duty to our motherland and to ourselves and to our future generations.

When the child is empowered by the parents, at various phases of growth, the child transforms into a responsible citizen. When the teacher is empowered with knowledge and experience, good young human beings with value systems take shape. When an individual or team is empowered with technology, transformation to higher potential for achievement is assured. When the leader of any institution empowers his or her people, leaders are born who can change the nation in multiple areas. When the women are empowered, society with stability gets assured. When the political leaders of the nation empower the people through visionary policies, the prosperity of the nation is certain. The medium for transformation to a developed India is the empowering at various levels with power of knowledge. A roadmap for realizing this vision of developed India is in front of us.

At this juncture, I recall a beautiful thought of Dr G.G. Swell, an eminent leader from the North-East: 'We must have a mental infrastructure. Mental infrastructure means sincerity of purpose, of vision, of purity of heart and mind.'

When I travel across our nation, when I hear the sound of waves of the three seas across the shores of my country, when I experience the breeze of wind from the mighty Himalayas, when I see the bio-diversity of the North-East and our islands and when I feel the warmth from the western desert, I hear the voice of the youth: 'When can I sing the song of India?' What can be the answer? I have so far interacted with over 50,000 schoolchildren over the past one year. I would like to share with you my answer to the urge of these children. If youth have to sing the song of India, India should become a developed country which is free from poverty, illiteracy and unemployment and is buoyant with economic prosperity, national security and internal harmony. To create this transformation we all have to resolve ourselves to work and sweat for the national development. I would like to share the song of youth, which I normally recite with these schoolchildren, at this juncture. I am very happy to see the children here representing the future generation. Through them I would like to convey the song of youth to all children of our country and the people.

As a young citizen of India

Armed with technology, knowledge and love for my nation,

I realize, small aim is a crime.

I will work and sweat for a great vision,

The vision of transforming India into a developed nation,

Powered by economic strength with value system.

I am one of the citizens of the billion;

Only the vision will ignite the billion souls.

It has entered into me;

The ignited soul compared to any resource

Is the most powerful resource

On the earth, above the earth and under the earth

I will keep the lamp of knowledge burning

To achieve the vision—Developed India.

If we work and sweat for the great vision with ignited minds, the transformation leading to the birth of a vibrant developed India will happen. This song, when sung in our own beautiful languages will unite our minds for action.

I pray to the Almighty: 'May the divine peace with beauty enter into our people; Happiness and good health blossom in our bodies, minds and souls.'

Jai Hind!

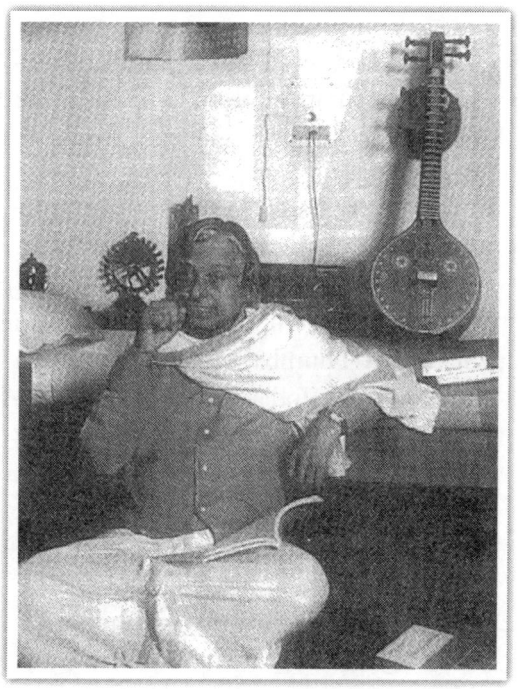

Chronology

1931	15 October, Avul Pakir Jainulabdeen Abdul Kalam born at Rameswaram, Tamil Nadu
1950	Joined St Joseph's College, Trichi for BSc degree
1954	Joined Madras Institute of Technology (MIT)
1958	Senior Scientific Assistant, DTDP (Air)
1962	INCOSPAR sets up Equatorial Rocket launching Station at Thumba
1963	21 November, India's first rocket – Nike-Apache launched
1964	Rohini-75 rocket launched
1968	Indian Rocket Society formed
1972	8 October, RATO system Sukhoi-l6 jet airplane tested
1974	Death of brother-in-law Jallaluddin
1976	Father Jainulabdeen dies at the age of 102. Mother passes away shortly after

1980	India's first Satellite Launch Vehicle – SLV-3 – launched
1981	25 January, President awards Padma Bhushan 31 May, SLV-3D launched
1982	Appointed Director, DRDL
1983	Missile development programme begins
1987	President awards Padma Vibhushan
1988	Second flight of Prithvi
1989	Agni missile launch
1990	Jadavpur University confers Doctor of Science degree
1991	Honorary Doctor of Science from IIT, Mumbai
1997	President awards Bharat Ratna, highest civilian award
1998	Scientific Advisor to the Government
2001	Resigns as Scientific Advisor
2002	18 June, Files nomination for President 15 July, Elected President 25 July, Takes Oath of Office as 11th President of India

A Bibliographic Note

Anyone interested in the life and work of President Kalam must visit the indispensable website *www.abdulkalam.com*. It contains information about President Kalam's life, activities and his vision of India, including copious extracts from his writings and interviews. The views of those who have been associated with Dr Kalam also figure. Questions for Dr Kalam can be left on the website, and will elicit a personal response from him. The site is regularly updated, and also provides links to other sites associated with Dr Kalam's work.

Wings Of Fire (Universities Press), written with Arun Tiwari, is Dr Kalam's own riveting and revealing account of his life. *Ignited Minds: Unleashing The Power Within India* (Viking Penguin), exceptionally well-written, is Dr Kalam's account of his interaction with students across the nation and throws much light on his life and thought. *India 2020* by A.P.J. Abdul Kalam and Y.S.